The Perfect Pet

First published in 2011
by Wayland

Text copyright © Liss Norton
Illustration copyright © Michael Garton

Wayland
338 Euston Road
London NW1 3BH

Wayland Australia
Level 17/207 Kent Street
Sydney, NSW 2000

Series Editor: Louise John
Editor: Katie Powell
Cover design: Paul Cherrill
Design: D.R.ink
Consultant: Shirley Bickler

A CIP catalogue record for this book is available from the British Library.

ISBN 9781526302687

Printed in China

Wayland is a division of Hachette Children's Books,
an Hachette UK Company

www.hachette.co.uk

The Perfect Pet

Written by Liss Norton
Illustrated by Michael Garton

WAYLAND

Creepy Castle stood on top of a creepy hill in the middle of a creepy forest. Two skeletons lived there. Their names were Skelly Nelly and Bony Tony.

One rainy day, Skelly Nelly and Bony Tony were playing in a room at the top of the castle tower.

"Look!" cried Skelly Nelly.
"I've found a bat!"

The bat was hanging from the roof, fast asleep.

"She's so cute," Skelly Nelly said. "Let's keep her as a pet

"A bat's a boring pet," said Bony Tony. "She'll sleep all day. We need a real pet. Something to guard Creepy Castle."

Bony Tony ran downstairs
to phone the zoo.

"I would like a pet," he said.
"Please send me a wolf."

The wolf arrived later that day.
It had thick grey fur, sharp white
teeth and angry yellow eyes.

"Just what we need!" said Bony
Tony. "A wolf is the perfect pet.
I'll call him Fang."

Bony Tony tied Fang up outside.

"Don't let anyone into Creepy Castle," he said.

Fang threw back his head and howled so loudly that Bony Tony's bones rattled.

"Perfect!" he cheered.

That afternoon, Bony Tony went to see Skelly Nelly in the tower.

She was reading a book, waiting for Batty to wake up.

"I'm going to buy Fang some food,"
said Bony Tony.

Outside, Fang was still guarding the castle.

He was howling loudly, frightening people away.

"Good boy!" said Bony Tony. "I'm off to get you some food. I'll be back soon."

When Bony Tony came back from the shops, Fang wouldn't let him in. He growled fiercely and bared his teeth.

"Let me in," commanded Bony Tony. "I live here."

drawbridge and charged at
Bony Tony.

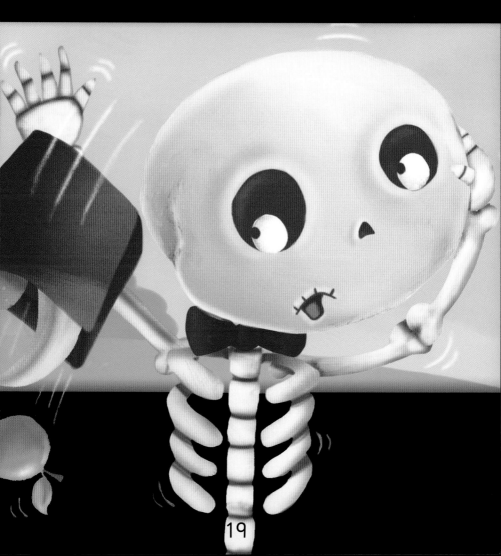

Bony Tony screamed and ran into the forest, climbing a tree just in time.

"Help! Skelly, help!" he shouted, but Fang howled so loudly that Skelly Nelly couldn't hear him.

When it got dark, Batty woke up.

"Hello, I'm Skelly Nelly," said
Skelly. "You can be my new pet.
I'm going to call you Batty."

Skelly Nelly was climbing down the stairs when suddenly, Batty flew out of the window.

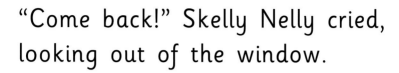

"Come back!" Skelly Nelly cried, looking out of the window.

Then she saw Bony Tony up in the tree, with Fang prowling beneath him.

"Oh, no!" cried Skelly Nelly, racing out of the castle.

At that moment, Batty swooped at Fang. She clawed at the wolf's head again and again.

Fang howled in pain and fled deep into the forest.

Batty chased him to make sure he didn't come back.

Bony Tony climbed down from the tree and raced to meet Skelly Nelly. "Are you OK?" she asked.

"I'm fine," he said. "Quick! Let's get back inside the castle."

Together, they crossed the drawbridge and ran up into the tower.

When Batty returned, Bony Tony stroked her gratefully.

"Well done, Batty!" he cried.

"So, you don't want a wolf as a pet any more?" asked Skelly Nelly.

"No, I don't!" Bony Tony replied. "Batty is the perfect pet!"

START READING is a series of highly enjoyable books for beginner readers. **The books have been carefully graded to match the Book Bands widely used in schools.** This enables readers to be sure they choose books that match their own reading ability.

Look out for the Band colour on the book in our Start Reading logo.

The Bands are:

Pink Band 1A & 1B

Red Band 2

Yellow Band 3

Blue Band 4

Green Band 5

Orange Band 6

Turquoise Band 7

Purple Band 8

Gold Band 9

START READING books can be read independently or shared with an adult. They promote the enjoyment of reading through satisfying stories, plays and non-fiction narratives, which are supported by fun illustrations and photographs.

Liss Norton loves growing organic fruit and vegetables in her garden in the Sussex countryside, as well as spending time with her grandchildren, Maddie, Arabella, Dominic and Theo. When she's not writing, gardening or grandchildren-ing, she likes visiting castles. One day she hopes to find a secret passage...

Michael Garton lives with his girlfriend Leanna and a dalmatian puppy called Kiba. He works from his creepy flat on the Wirral in England (it's not quite a castle yet but he's saving up for one). He has been illustrating children's books since 2004 and thinks that everyone should have as many creepy experiences as possible.